Paddington
at the
Rainbow's End

First published in paperback in Great Britain by HarperCollins Children's Books in 2009
Board book edition published in 2016
This edition published as part of a set in 2017

1 3 5 7 9 10 8 6 4 2

ISBN: 978-0-00-796825-1

HarperCollins Children's Books is a division of HarperCollins Publishers Ltd.

Text copyright © Michael Bond 2009
Illustrations copyright © R. W. Alley 2009

Visit our website at: www.harpercollins.co.uk

Printed in China

Michael Bond
Paddington
at the
Rainbow's End

Illustrated by R. W. Alley

HarperCollins *Children's Books*

One morning Paddington
saw a rainbow in the sky.
It didn't last long, so
he went out shopping
to see how many
different colours he
could find for himself.

Sure enough, he hadn't gone very far before the driver of a big, red bus caught sight of his hat and gave a friendly toot. Paddington raised his hat in return.

Then, at the bakers,
he found some buns
which were exactly
the same brown as
his basket on wheels.

In the market there were
bunches of bananas that
were as bright and clean
as his yellow boots.

And there were lots
of blue flowers. One
of them was the same
colour as his duffle coat.

Special Price

Best of all… Paddington
licked his lips when he
came across some jars
of orange marmalade.

On his way home,
he stopped to look up
at the sky. The sun had
almost gone, and in its
place there were lots
of dark grey clouds.

Paddington hurried on his way. He was glad he had his black umbrella. It helped keep his buns dry.

Another nice thing about
colours was having a
green front door. It
meant he never went
to the wrong house
by mistake.

When he was indoors,
Paddington found a
sheet of white paper
and carefully drew all
the things he had seen
that morning, so that
he could colour them
in with crayons.

But when he looked
for an orange crayon
he couldn't find one
anywhere. He felt hungry
after all his shopping and
the sight of the empty
space gave him an idea.

He dipped his paw into
the jar of marmalade.
"Now I know why I like
orange best," he said,
licking his paw clean.
"There's no other colour
quite like it."

Look out for more fantastic books about Paddington!

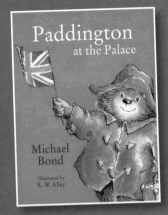

Paddington
at the Palace

Michael
Bond

Illustrated by
R. W. Alley

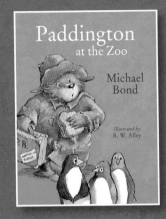

Paddington
at the Zoo

Michael
Bond

Illustrated by
R. W. Alley

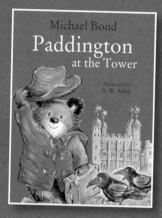

Michael Bond
Paddington
at the Tower

Illustrated by
R. W. Alley

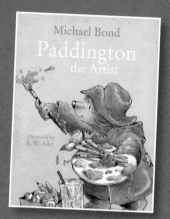

Michael Bond
Paddington
the Artist

Illustrated by
R. W. Alley

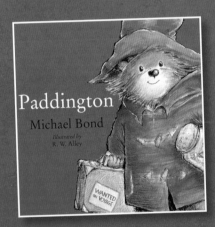

Paddington
Michael Bond

Illustrated by
R. W. Alley

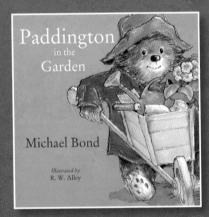

Paddington
in the
Garden

Michael Bond

Illustrated by
R. W. Alley

Michael Bond
Paddington
and the
Grand Tour

Illustrated by R. W. Alley

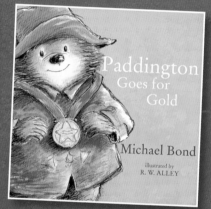

Paddington
Goes for
Gold

Michael Bond

illustrated by
R. W. ALLEY

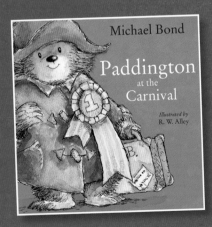

Michael Bond
Paddington
at the
Carnival

Illustrated by
R. W. Alley

Michael Bond
Paddington
and the
Christmas
Surprise

Illustrated by R. W. ALLEY

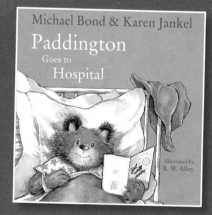

Michael Bond & Karen Jankel
Paddington
Goes to
Hospital

Illustrated by
R. W. Alley

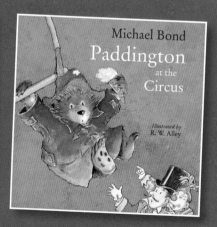

Michael Bond
Paddington
at the
Circus

Illustrated by
R. W. Alley

HarperCollins *Children's Books*